THE BIG COMFY COUCH™

Night Owl Loonette

Written by **Gavin Jackson**

Illustrated by **Richard Kolding**

TIME LIFE **Kids**

**ALEXANDRIA,
VIRGINIA**

The sun was just going down over Clowntown, but on the Big Comfy Couch, Loonette the clown was very busy. Tomorrow she was having a costume party, and there were so many things to get ready.

"Oh, Molly!" Loonette said to her best friend. "Here are some great costumes for our guests. Let's try them on. Want to?"

All Molly wanted to try on were her pajamas. It was bedtime.

"Oh, Molly, you are such a sleepyhead," Loonette said. "Not me. I'm a night owl."

Little dolls need their sleep, but night owls stay awake all night long. So Loonette tiptoed over to Miss Loonette's Dance Academy to try on costumes with Roberto—and dance, of course.

But Roberto could not help with the party plans, and neither could the Foley Family. Andy and his mom and dad were all tucked into their cozy little dollhouse beds.

"Someclown must want to stay up all night with me to get this party ready," thought Loonette. "I know—Granny!"

The moon was bright as Loonette headed for Granny Garbanzo's garden. At that very moment, Granny stuck her head out of her cart window.

"Yoicks!" she said to her cat, Snicklefritz. "What are you doing outside? It's bedtime." Then she saw Loonette. "It's not my bedtime, Granny," Loonette called. "I'm a night owl. I'm going to stay up all night long."

Granny laughed and said, "Home you go, Loonetka, dear. If you don't sleep, you'll be too tired for your party tomorrow."

But Loonette did not believe what Granny said. As she headed back to the Big Comfy Couch, she said loudly, "I *am* a night owl."

"Hoo?" called an old owl from the top of a tree.

"Me. Loonette the clown. You're so lucky. You get to stay up every night. I'm going to stay up tonight, even if all my friends are asleep."

From a distance Loonette
heard some happy music.
It was coming from
Clowntown. This gave
her an idea. She got her
telescope from beneath
the cushions of the Big
Comfy Couch. Then she
aimed the telescope right
toward Clowntown.

"If I can find out where
that music is coming
from," she said, "maybe I
can find someclown to
stay up with me."

First Loonette aimed the telescope at Major Bedhead's tilted little cottage. Through his open window, with the moonlight streaming in, she could see him sleeping.

"I guess Major Bedhead can't stay up with me," Loonette told herself.

Next Loonette aimed the telescope at the sturdy little
house that Wobbly had built for himself.
The light was on by his door, and his
carriage was leaning against the
house, piled with doodads and
whatnots. Through Wobbly's open
window, she could see
him sleeping too.

"I guess Wobbly can't
stay up with me either,"
Loonette told herself.

By that time the music had stopped.

"I guess those clowns making the music are not night owls after all," Loonette said. "But I am. I'm staying up all night."

Loonette let out a big yawn and rubbed her eyes. But she would not go to sleep.

Loonette tried on all the
costumes, except a tiny
one that looked as if it
would fit Molly.

Then she found
some of her own
musical instruments
in the couch.

Finally, she made
enough prune-and-
pickle sandwiches to
feed all her friends.

The next afternoon all of Loonette's friends—and even her
Auntie Macassar—came to her party. They loved
wearing the costumes. They had fun playing clowny music.
And they gobbled up every last prune-and-pickle sandwich.

After a while, Major Bedhead noticed something was
wrong. "Has anyclown seen Loonette?" he asked.

But noclown had seen her.

"Oh, dear," said Granny. "We must go find her."

Auntie Macassar spotted Loonette leaning against a wheel of Granny's cart, fast asleep.

"Poor dear Loonetka," said Granny with a sigh. "She is so tired from staying up all night that she can't keep awake at her own party. I guess little clowns were just not meant to be night owls!"

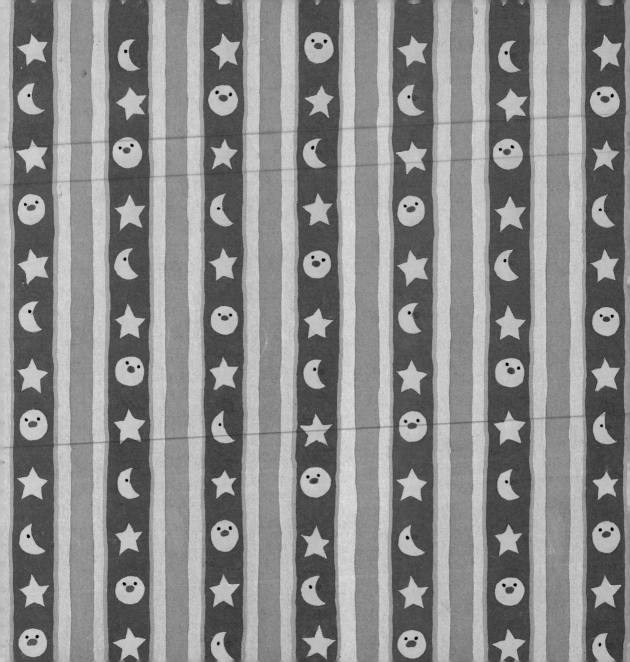